INVASION OF THE JUNKYARD HOG

INVASION OF THE JUNKYARD HOG

by **Bill Doyle**

illustrated by **Scott Altmann**

A STEPPING STONE BOOK™

Random House 🏠 New York

To five magical friends from 1808
—B.D.
For Addie, Dylan, and Melanie
—S.A.

This is a work of fiction. Names, characters, places, and incidents either are the product of the author's imagination or are used fictitiously. Any resemblance to actual persons, living or dead, events, or locales is entirely coincidental.

Text copyright © 2014 by Bill Doyle
Cover art and interior illustrations copyright © 2014 by Scott Altmann
All rights reserved. Published in the United States by Random House Children's Books, a division of Random House LLC, a Penguin Random House Company, New York.
Random House and the colophon are registered trademarks and A Stepping Stone Book and the colophon are trademarks of Random House LLC.

Visit us on the Web!
SteppingStonesBooks.com
randomhouse.com/kids

Educators and librarians, for a variety of teaching tools,
visit us at RHTeachersLibrarians.com

Library of Congress Cataloging-in-Publication Data
Doyle, Bill H.
Invasion of the junkyard hog / by Bill Doyle ; illustrated by Scott Altmann.
pages   cm.
"A Stepping Stone book."
Summary: Nine-year-old cousins Keats and Henry must find a lost magical compass before a destructive magic-sniffing junkyard hog finds it first.
ISBN 978-0-385-37130-8 (pbk.) — ISBN 978-0-385-37131-5 (lib. bdg.) —
ISBN 978-0-385-37132-2 (ebook)
[1. Magic—Fiction. 2. Pigs—Fiction. 3. Cousins—Fiction.]
I. Altmann, Scott, illustrator. II. Title.
PZ7.D7725In 2014   [Fic]—dc23   2013008373
Printed in the United States of America
10 9 8 7 6 5 4 3 2 1

CONTENTS

1

WAND WANTED

"HENRY!" KEATS SHOUTED for his cousin. "Help! I'm going to fall!"

Keats was alone in his backyard on Tangle-wood Lane. Normally that wouldn't be a problem. But he was teetering on a pair of wooden stilts—four feet off the ground.

Each time Keats tried to step off, one stilt slid away from the other. It was like standing on two giant chopsticks . . . on ice.

This isn't my fault! Keats thought. He'd never be stuck up here if he didn't have so much free time. The library was closed this week for a summer cleaning. And he'd read all his own books at least twice.

So when he'd spotted the stilts next to the patio door, he'd climbed up on them. What else was he supposed to do?

Wobbling even more, he shouted, "Henry!" Keats's cousin lived next door, but he was nowhere in sight. Keats tried again, even louder. "Help!"

Suddenly Henry stepped out from behind a tree. The surprise almost knocked Keats off balance. Had Henry been back there watching the whole time?

"What's *up*, cuz?" Henry was nine years old, just like Keats, and usually a couple inches taller. Now he grinned up at Keats. "Huh," he said. "I guess Slippery Stilts aren't my World's Greatest Plan after all."

Keats groaned. "You and your crazy World's Greatest Plans! Just get me off these things!"

"Hmmm." Henry pretended to study the stilts. "Oh, I know what would do the trick," he said, and snapped his fingers. "A magic wand!"

"Ugh!" Keats should have known Henry would say that.

Earlier that summer, the cousins had taken on odd jobs for a magician named Mr. Cigam. As a reward, Mr. Cigam had given them a magic wand. Henry wanted to use it all the time for his nutty ideas. First he thought of selling roller skates for cats. Then he came up with a plan to knit leashes for worms. Finally Keats had hidden the wand under his bed.

"You left these stilts there on purpose!" Keats said. He swayed back and forth. "You knew I'd need help. You just want the wand!"

"No way!" Henry was scratching his chin. That was a sure sign he wasn't being honest. "I guess I'll go find another way to get you down."

Keats couldn't believe it. Henry was leaving!

"Henry!" Keats shouted. "Wait!"

"Just kidding," Henry said, turning back. "If you really need help . . ."

That did it. Keats wasn't as good at athletic stuff as Henry. Still he wasn't a total klutz. "Never mind," he said. "I'll do it myself."

Big mistake. The instant Keats lifted one foot off a stilt, the other stilt slipped across the patio. He tried to catch himself, but now both stilts were sliding. He felt like a moving goalpost.

"Hang on, Keats!" Henry moved fast, just

not fast enough. The stilts slid off the patio. They hit the grass and stopped . . . but Keats kept moving.

FLA—pinggg!

He flew sideways through the air, as if flicked by a giant finger. The stilts clattered to the patio. Keats braced himself to smack into the ground.

Instead, with a *whoosh,* he sank shoulder first into two pillowy garbage bags. "What . . . ?" he gasped, leaning on one elbow.

Henry laughed. "I put out bags of grass clippings and leaves this morning, in case you fell." He jumped, spun in the air, and landed on a bag next to Keats. "You didn't think I'd *leaf* my best friend hanging, did you?"

Keats whacked Henry's shoulder and opened his mouth—

Keeeeee! A high-pitched shriek cut him off.

"Did you do that?" Henry asked, eyes wide.

Keats shook his head.

Eeettsss! A different sound, just as piercing, filled the air. "Is that inside my house?" Keats said.

The cousins hopped to their feet. They ran through the patio door and into the living room. The house was empty. Both their moms were at work at the Purple Rabbit Market.

Dhenn!

"That came from the basement!" Henry said.

The cousins rushed through the kitchen and down the stairs. In the lead, Henry suddenly stopped. "Wait a second, Keats!" he warned.

Too late. Keats bumped into him, and they fell onto the basement's orange shag carpet.

Down there, new noises blared and blasted

all around them. Keats felt like he'd tumbled into the middle of a band playing the world's weirdest music.

Eeettsss!

"It's the radiator!" Keats said. He climbed to his feet and pointed to an old heater in the corner.

Dhenn!

"No," Henry said. "It's the blow-up dinosaur!" He pointed to the shelf of beach toys.

Reeee!

Keats looked around, his stomach flipflopping. "The sounds are coming from *everywhere.*"

It was true. Anything with air inside—from a life jacket to a football—was hissing, sizzling, or whistling. It was like they were teapots filled with boiling water. And the noises were getting louder.

"Let's get out of here!" Henry said. He pulled Keats toward the stairs, but they didn't get far. Jets of steam blasted out of the holes in a watering can. They hit Keats's arm.

"Hey!" he shouted. Good thing he was wearing his jacket.

The steam pushed the cousins into the middle of the room. Henry ducked under the steam and snatched the plastic lid off a big tub of old magazines.

"This can be our shield!" Henry yelled. "Make a run for the stairs!"

But Keats didn't move. "Hold on," he said. "There's something strange about the sounds. Listen!"

Henry stood still as the air whistled and hissed.

Keee! Eeettsss! Annnn! Dhenn! Reeee!

"You're right!" Henry's eyes went wide.

"When you put the noises together, it sounds like *Keats and Henry*!"

"This could be magic," Keats said. He moved a few steps to his left and Henry followed. In the exact center of the room, the weird sounds clicked into place. The cousins heard a message made up of mismatched notes.

Keats and Henry,

Our stepbrother is Archibald Cigam.
He suggested we contact you. We have a
magical job for you today at the Tophat
Junkyard. Will you accept?

Yours sincerely,

Lillian and Beatrice Cigam

Right away, the message started over. The
hot air shrieked even louder around them.
Soon not even the plastic lid would protect
them from the blasting steam.

"What should we do?" Keats yelled. Henry
shouted something back, but Keats couldn't
hear over all the noise.

If the steam got even stronger next time
the message played, they'd be in big trouble.
When the message got to "Will you accept?"
Henry nudged Keats.

The cousins shouted at the same time, "Yes! We accept!"

Click! Like someone had flipped a switch, the shrieking and steam stopped. Keats's ears rang as he and Henry caught their breath.

"Looks like we have another job," Henry said finally. "And, Keats, this time—"

"Okay, okay," Keats agreed, knowing what Henry was about to say. "This time we're bringing the wand!"

2

BEWARE OF THE HOG

THE COUSINS HOPPED on their bikes and took off toward Main Street. The Tophat Junkyard sat outside town on the other side of Steep Cliff Hill.

"Pick up the pace, Keats," Henry said. "My mom left chicken in the fridge. I want to be back home for lunch!"

"Time for turbo speed, Roget!" Keats called to his bike. He struggled to keep up with

Henry, especially on the bigger hills. Henry made biking uphill look easy, even wearing his backpack.

The cousins pedaled by the last of the houses in town, past the park, and up one more long hill. Finally the road flattened out. A twenty-foot-high fence stretched along the left side for at least half a mile.

Henry slowed down. "That's the junkyard," he said. "But how do we get inside?"

"There must . . . be a gate . . . ," Keats said, still huffing.

Sure enough, up ahead a short driveway led to a closed metal gate. A sign with big block letters had been welded to the gate. It read BEWARE OF THE HOG.

"Hog?" Henry chuckled. "Looks like some-one could use one of your dictionaries, Keats."

The cousins got off their bikes, and Keats

pushed the gate. It moved a few inches, but a thick chain lock held it shut. "Hello!" he shouted through the narrow opening.

No one answered. All Keats heard was the wind blowing through the cornfield across the road.

Henry gave the gate a shove, too. "It won't budge," he said. "And our bikes won't fit through the crack. We'll have to leave them here." When Keats hesitated, Henry sighed. "Don't worry. Roget will be fine."

Turning his body to squeeze through the gate, Henry slipped into the junkyard first. "Stunner," Keats heard him say. "Keats, you've got to see this!"

Keats followed, squirming his way inside. When he took a quick look around, his heartbeat kicked up.

The cousins stood on a dirt path wide

enough for a dump truck. On either side, two solid walls of junk soared into the air.

Stacks of rusting washing machines loomed next to heaps of busted TVs. Piles of broken lawn mowers sat side by side with towers of stoves, lamps, and toilets.

"Whoa," Keats breathed. "This is the second-coolest place I've ever seen."

Henry laughed. "Yeah, but the *library*

doesn't have one of those." He pointed to a
bulldozer with a giant scooper. It was parked
next to a two-story-high crane that dangled a
magnet the size of a small car.

Keats whistled. "Amazing! So do you think
Mr. Cigam's stepsisters are in there?" He
nodded toward a large shed farther up the
path. A sign on its door read OFFICE.

"One way to find out!" Henry said.

As they started walking, a shadow rippled on the ground in front of them. Something passed between them and the sun, like a cloud or a giant bird. But when Keats looked up, he didn't see anything.

For some reason, Keats shivered. "Let's keep moving," he said. They picked up speed on the dusty path to the windowless shed. When Henry raised a hand to knock on the tin door, it creaked open. A woman's wrinkled face, topped by a wild beehive of silver hair, appeared. "Olleh!" she chirped.

Another, slightly older face joined the first. "She meant to say *hello*," the second woman said. "I'm Beatrice, and this is my sister, Lillian. We're so pleased you gentlemen got our message. Well, come in. Come in!"

The sisters backed into the shed. Keats gave Henry a look, but Henry just shrugged.

Together they went through the door. Inside the small room, sunlight shone through tiny cracks in the metal ceiling.

Now that he could see the sisters better, Keats decided they were about his grandma's age. They wore leather jackets over ball gowns. It was as if they had left a fancy party to take a motorcycle ride.

But the strangest thing about the sisters? They were walking backward and sideways.

"Are you okay?" Keats asked as Beatrice backed into a coatrack.

"Enif, enif," Lillian said.

Keats was about to ask what she meant when Beatrice said, "No reason to lie, Lillian dear." Turning to the cousins, she added, "No, we're not *fine*. Take a seat, gentlemen."

The cousins sat down on stools at a workbench piled high with boat propellers.

"Do you own a compass?" Beatrice asked.

"Uh, sure," Keats said, thrown by the out-of-the-blue question. "My dad's car has one so we know what direction we're heading in."

"Well, my sister and I had a compass, too," Beatrice said. "We were making spells with it when something went wrong."

Keats shot Henry a look that said, *See what playing with magic can do?*

Henry rolled his eyes. "What happened?" he asked the sisters.

Beatrice sighed. "We cast a dizziness spell. It gave us that wonderful feeling you get when you spin around and around and around."

Lillian clapped her hands happily at the memory.

"But before we could set things right," Beatrice went on, "our stepbrother Archibald accidentally threw the compass into a box of

old toys. He dumped the box somewhere in this junkyard."

"Oh!" Keats said. "So without the compass, you've lost your sense of direction?"

Beatrice nodded. "We don't know which way is what! Poor Lillian even talks backward." She sighed. "That's better, of course, than talking sideways. Or diagonally."

"Lufwa!" Lillian said, bumping into her sister.

"So we bought the junkyard. We closed it and moved here to look for the compass," Beatrice explained. "We even cast a spell on a hog to help us. Hogs can sniff out things, you know. But that went . . . a little wrong."

Keats looked more closely at her faded dress. "How long have you been here?"

"Shtnom!" Lillian chirped.

"Yes, *months*," Beatrice said. "That's why we need you gentlemen to find the compass. We used the last of our magic to get in touch with you."

"You're out of magic?" Henry said. "No problem." He slipped off his backpack and reached inside. "Try this."

Henry held out the wand to the sisters.

· 22 ·

Lillian took one look at the goofy rod with the lightbulb on top and ran backward into the wall. "On!" she shouted.

"Oh, it's not *on*," Henry said, waving the wand around. "We don't even know if it still works or—"

"Yooodooohooo!" A yodel came from outside. Then a whooshing noise. Since there were no windows in the shed, Keats couldn't see what was making the sounds.

Beatrice yelled, "Put the wand away!"

Before Henry could . . . *WHAM!* Something slammed into the side of the shed.

The floor tilted, and Henry and Keats were tossed off their stools. Henry held on to the wand but dropped the backpack. It tumbled past the sisters' feet as they rushed backward and sideways in a panic.

"Wh-what's happening?" Keats sputtered

as the building was struck a second time.

WHAM!

This time the entire shed lifted off the ground. Was it going to flip over? The propellers slid off the table in a series of crashes.

Lillian yelled, "Goh!"

"It's the flying junkyard *hog*!" Beatrice shouted to the cousins.

A tusk as long as an elephant's speared the wall from the outside. It sliced through the metal like a can opener through a tin of tuna.

"The hog you brought here can *fly*?" Henry asked, leaping out of the way as a tool cabinet fell over.

"Now it can!" Beatrice said. "The junkyard is filled with magical rubbish. The hog found a flying charm that gave it wings!"

The hog's other tusk poked through the wall and carved upward, lifting the shed higher.

Keats held on to the leg of the workbench to keep from sliding across the floor. "What does it want?" he yelled above the screeching of tearing metal.

"It smells the magic of the wand!" Beatrice shouted. "Put it back in the bag!"

Scrambling, Keats snatched the backpack and tossed it to Henry. The tusks were cutting straight lines up to the ceiling. Soon the entire wall would peel open.

"Yrruh!" Lillian shouted.

"*Hurry!*" Beatrice cried.

Henry stuffed the wand inside the bag and zipped it shut. The instant the bag closed, everything went quiet. The tusks froze and then slid slowly back out through the wall.

Freed, the tilted shed rocked to the ground with a *wa-oomph*. Keats's teeth clicked together as he was tossed to the floor again.

"What's—" Henry started to ask, but Lillian held up a hand.

"*Hhhs,*" she said.

A loud, wet sniff came from outside the holes in the wall. Keats caught sight of a huge brown hairy nostril. Then the nose pulled out of view.

Keats heard flapping sounds. It was as if a giant bird were flying away.

"Well, that was—" Beatrice started to say, and Lillian finished for her, "Nuf."

3

CHOPPER ZONE

KEATS DIDN'T DARE move from his spot on the floor for a couple seconds. Was the junkyard hog coming back?

"Uh, right . . . *fun*," Henry finally said. He gave Keats a hand up. Shaken, Keats steered clear of the long jagged hole in the wall.

"Oh, don't worry!" Beatrice said. "The hog is probably searching for more magical items. It really wants the compass. Once it finds that, the spell we cast to keep the hog in the junk-yard will be broken. It can fly off to any part of the world it likes. That's why you have to find the compass first!"

"Okaaay," Henry said. His eyes had gotten wider and wider as Beatrice spoke. "You know what, Keats? It's my World's Greatest Plan that we go get lunch. Now. We can come back later." He was scratching his chin.

"Sure," Keats pretended to agree. Getting attacked by a flying hog wasn't his idea of a good way to spend a summer morning. Still he felt a little guilty. He asked the sisters, "Maybe Mr. Cigam could help you find the compass?"

"Archibald?" Beatrice scoffed. "I don't know if you've noticed, dear, but he's rather mixed up lately."

"Yeah, we've definitely noticed," Henry said.

Lillian must have sensed they meant to leave for good. "Esaelp!" she said.

"*Please,*" Beatrice said. "Just keep the wand zipped up tight and the hog won't smell it. If you don't find the compass, we'll be stuck here forever."

"Reverof," Lillian said sadly.

Shaking his head, Henry said, "This place is huge. Where would we start looking?"

The sisters laughed. "You're asking *us* for directions?" Beatrice said.

"Syot!" Lillian chirped.

"True," Beatrice said with a nod. "Archibald brought the compass here with old *toys.* You could start in the junkyard's toy zone. It's right on the path. You can't miss it."

The sisters were bumping Henry and Keats toward the door. After several tries, Lillian opened it.

"Which path?" Henry asked.

"There's only one," Beatrice answered. "It makes a big circle through the junkyard. If you follow it, you'll end up back here. Just stay away from the center."

"Wait . . . why?" Keats asked, but the sisters were pushing them through the doorway.

"Don't worry," Beatrice said. "When you find the compass, stop the spinning needle. We'll come to you!"

With that she closed the door. The cousins heard the lock turn from inside. Henry and Keats stood facing the shack.

"Hold on," Keats said, dazed. "What just happened?"

"I think we agreed to find a magic compass in a huge junkyard that's been invaded by a flying hog," Henry said. He turned toward the junkyard gate. "But there's our way out."

More banging came from inside the shed. Keats could imagine the sisters bumping into each other.

Keats sighed. "We have to help them, Henry." He stared up into the clear, sunny sky. "Besides, there's no sign of the hog."

"Chicken is great for lunch, but who wants to be one?" Henry said. He winked at Keats. "All right. We'll do it. We'll just stay on the path."

Side by side, the cousins walked away from the shed, deeper into the junkyard. The path curved through walls of tubs, sinks, and toilets.

"This must be the bathroom junk," Keats said. Then he pointed to piles of dishwashers, stoves, and microwaves up ahead. "And there's the kitchen area."

"What's in here?" Keats stopped to look in a steel bin next to the path.

Henry lifted out a handful of cabinet knobs. "They must strip everything down and sort the parts," he said. He tossed the knobs back in the bin and wiped his hands on his pants.

Keats opened the next bin. It was filled with showerheads.

"The sisters forgot to tell us what the compass looks like," Keats said as he stood on his toes to peek inside.

"Not to worry," Henry said. "I bet we'll know it when we see it. It's bound to be pretty strange!"

They hiked through a canyon of tractor mowers. After that came busted red wagons, rusty swing sets, and broken bicycle frames.

"I think we've entered the toy zone," Keats said.

Henry spotted something in the dirt. "Hoofprints, cuz!" he cried happily. "The junkyard hog has been here!"

Glancing up at the sky, Keats gasped. "Why do you sound like you want to throw a party?"

"The hog can smell magic, right?" Henry said. "Maybe he was on the scent of the magic compass."

They followed the tracks to a clump of half-buried toys next to the wall of wagons.

From the hoof marks everywhere, it was

clear the hog had been digging up the toys. Keats saw the tail of a rocking horse, the head and arms of a monkey holding cymbals, and two blades from a remote-control helicopter.

Closer to the wall, the hog had dug a deeper hole.

Henry crouched down next to it. "I wonder what the hog was after in here. . . ." He reached inside and felt around with his hand. "A-ha!" he said.

Keats's hopes shot up. "Is it the compass?"

Henry pulled his hand out. Instead of a compass, he was gripping a rusty toy dog the size of a loaf of bread. It had metal springs for legs and a steel tube for a body. Its two ears looked like flattened soda cans. A small wrench was clamped in its mouth like a bone.

"Check it out." Henry ran his finger along

the side of the toy. Someone had scratched PROPERTY OF A. CIGAM in the metal.

"A. Cigam?" Henry said. "That must be Mr. Cigam! We found his old toys!"

Keats shook his head. Something didn't make sense here. "Why would he bury them?" he asked.

Shrugging, Henry flipped the toy's power switch. Nothing happened. "Looks like the battery is dead." Henry gave the dog a shake. Some rust fell off.

Keats squinted. "There's something else written on the battery compartment."

"You're right," Henry said. "It says, *Better bet*—" He stopped to wipe off a clump of dirt.

As Henry took a breath to keep reading, Keats had a sinking feeling in his stomach. Mr. Cigam was a magician. This could be a spell. "Wait, Henry!" he said.

Too late. Henry read, *"Better bet this bat-tered battery will be better yet."*

There was a sizzling sound, then—

Boing!

The toy dog's brown marble eyes flew open. It squirmed out of Henry's hands, and its rusty legs hit the ground with a creaky bounce.

"Stunner," Henry said. But it wasn't just the dog that came to life. Every toy within the

sound of Henry's voice was moving. The rocking horse's tail twitched. The monkey's head spun. And between the cousins and the path, the blades of the half-buried helicopter waggled in the dirt.

"What's going on?" Henry said. "I didn't use the wand!"

"It must be a wandless spell!" Keats said. "It made dead batteries work again."

The toy dog started yapping with a tinny bark and bouncing in circles. Then it clattered off down the path.

ZINK! The helicopter freed itself, popping up out of the ground. The toy's blades spun quickly into a blur. It hovered, then lurched sideways.

Now, inches off the ground, the rotor whirled toward Henry and Keats like a giant ceiling fan.

"What kind of toy is *that*?" Henry asked.

"One that you'd want to bury in a junk-yard," Keats said. "That's why Mr. Cigam dug holes for all this stuff!"

The cousins backed up between two bins of metal parts. Soon they were pressed up against the wall of red wagons.

The helicopter had them trapped. Henry found a rock by his feet and threw it at the toy. With a few sparks, the blades cracked the rock into pieces and kept spinning.

Henry and Keats tried to squeeze past the helicopter one way and then the other. But it flew back and forth, blocking them.

The blades were fifteen feet from them and coming closer each second.

"We need to do something fast!" Henry shouted. "Try the wand, Keats!"

Desperate, Keats unzipped the backpack

on Henry's back and pulled out the wand.

"Quick!" Henry said. "Make up a spell!"

Keats's mind raced. "Um, halt that helicopter, so it won't, uh . . ." He trailed off. "I can't think of a word that rhymes with *helicopter*!"

"Magic doesn't have to be perfect!" Henry said as the blades sliced closer, blowing back their hair. "Say anything!"

Keats was still drawing a blank. He just waved the wand at the whirling rotor. "I need a rhyme!" he shouted. "Nothing is happening!"

"Wrong," Henry said. "Look!"

He pointed up, past the sideways helicopter. The blue sky wasn't empty anymore. A creature the size of a couch with giant flapping wings blotted out the sun.

The flying hog was heading straight at them.

4

AVALANCHE!

AS IT FLEW closer, the cousins got their first good look at the junkyard hog.

"Holy moly," Keats whispered.

It was like a farm hog inflated to ten times its normal size. Brown-feathered wings had grown on both sides of the hog's back. Clumps of black hair and warts sprouted from its pink skin and around its red eyes. But what really caught Keats's attention were the sharp white tusks on either side of its long snout.

"Put the wand away!" Henry shouted. Keats shoved the wand into the backpack and zipped it up.

The hog circled once. Then it swooped in about thirty feet over their heads.

They had to escape, but there was nowhere to run. The helicopter still had them trapped.

"Yooodooohooo!" the hog yodeled. As Keats looked up, the hog's wings folded back against its body. It plummeted at them.

"Incoming!" Henry cried.

The hog missile was moving so fast, the pink skin rippled on its face. Keats could tell its body wasn't made for flying. Instead of a straight line, the hog dive-bombed on a wobbly course.

"I have an idea!" Henry said. He jerked one way and then another. The helicopter zigged and zagged with him. Henry faked going right. The blades went right. . . .

"Now!" Henry pulled Keats forward and to the left. Keats felt the blades bite into the air inches from his body. The cousins barely slipped between the bin and the helicopter.

Then everything seemed to happen at once. The flying hog tried to change course in midair, aiming for the cousins. It wobbled and—

Sping!

The hog nicked the back of one of the blades. The helicopter rammed into the dirt and got stuck again.

The impact sent the junkyard hog out of control. It spiraled through the air and into the wall of wagons.

CRASH!

Keats glanced back while he ran. The hog

thudded onto the spot right where the cousins had been. With a huge snort, it shook itself, sending dirt flying. Then, spreading its wings, it rose into the air again.

"The hog's coming back!" Keats said. "Keep moving!"

The cousins scrambled farther down the path. Behind them, the wall of wagons made a creaking sound. With a *snap*, it started to collapse.

"Avalanche!" Henry shouted. He and Keats ducked behind a bin of broken lamp stands.

The wall of red wagons crashed over the path like a tidal wave. With a clamor that hurt Keats's ears, the wagons buried the helicopter and the rest of Mr. Cigam's toys.

But the chaos didn't end there. Like dominoes, the wagons knocked into the wall of bikes, which fell into the swing sets. Dirt

swirled and shot into the air as everything came smashing down.

And then the junkyard was quiet.

Breathing hard, the cousins stared at the disaster. Slowly the dust clouds settled. Keats searched the sky for the hog. It was gone . . . for now.

"I have to say I'm rethinking this job,"

Henry murmured. "Being a chicken is sounding better and better."

Keats was still stunned. "That hog only wanted the wand," he said softly. "Not us, or the magic toys."

"Why are we just standing here?" Henry said, throwing up his hands. "This is nuts!"

Keats nodded and snapped out of it. "When

you're right, you're right," he said. "Let's get our bikes and go home. The sisters will have to find the compass another way."

The cousins headed back toward the toy zone. A twenty-foot mountain of caved-in wagons and bikes and swing sets blocked the path.

"We can climb over," Henry said. But it wasn't as easy as it looked. Keats put his foot on a bike frame to step over a swing set. His foot slipped and the junk higher up tumbled toward him. The handle of a wagon whacked into his shoe.

"Ouch!" Keats said. He tried again. Each time he set off mini junk slides.

"Whoa!" Henry said. "This is dangerous."

"We can't get back," Keats said miserably. "We're stuck."

Henry shook his head. "The path is one big

circle, right? We can keep going around until we come back to the front gate. Who knows? We might find a shortcut on the way."

Keats looked at the sky. Still no sign of the hog. "Okay," he said with a nod. After all, what choice did they have?

They took the path away from the destroyed toy zone and sped through the restaurant and movie theater areas. Giant popcorn makers that still smelled like fake butter were piled high.

"So what does magic smell like to the flying hog?" Henry asked. "Popcorn, maybe?"

Keats shrugged. Henry was trying to distract him from the hog. "I don't know," he said.

"Must smell like something good," Henry said. "For me, it'd be like grassy football cleats. For you, I bet it'd be the smell you get when you flip the pages of an old book."

This actually made Keats smile. "Good one, Henry."

The cousins walked and walked. Soon the walls of junk were a blur of rusty machines and strange parts. They didn't stop to look in any of the bins. Keats just wanted to get out of there.

Henry asked, "Do you think the compass was buried back there under the wagons?"

Keats shook his head. "The hog gave up digging around the toys," he said. "And if it had found the compass, the sisters said it would have flown away. No, I bet the compass is still somewhere in the junkyard."

Just then the hairs on the back of Keats's neck stood on end. He slowed down.

"What is it, Keats?" Henry asked.

"Shhh," Keats whispered. "Something is following us."

"I know." Henry chuckled. "It's called bad luck."

Fa-ping. A metallic shuffling noise came from the nearby pile of coffeemakers. Keats's stomach flip-flopped.

"Don't panic," Henry said. "Maybe it's a big mouse?"

Crash! A coffee can lid rolled across the path like a tumbleweed. Something had knocked it loose.

"A *very* big mouse?" Henry added.

"It could be the hog," Keats whispered. He checked to make sure the wand was still zipped up tight.

Henry shook his head. "I don't think sneak-iness is a huge thing with the hog." He turned and called back, "Hello? Who's there?"

No answer. Suddenly Keats didn't want to find out who—or what—it was.

The cousins moved ahead more quickly. The noise trailed behind them. Soon Henry and Keats were running. Still the noise got closer. Whatever was making it would catch up to them in just a few seconds.

They dashed around a sharp turn and nearly slammed into eight big blue metal barrels.

"We can't outrun it," Henry said. "We have to hide until it goes past." He tipped an empty barrel back so Keats could see the bottom was missing.

"There's not room in there for both of us," Keats said.

"You get inside this one," Henry said. "And I'll take that one. Hurry!"

Keats nodded. As Henry tilted up his own barrel, Keats crawled under the lip of the other one. Inside, tiny dots of light came through the rusted top.

"Henry?" Keats whispered.

"Shhh, it's coming," Henry said.

There was a clanking sound. Keats held his breath. Suddenly he heard Henry shout, "A-ha!"

Henry was in trouble! Keats had to help! He lifted the bottom of the barrel too fast, and the whole thing toppled over. It rolled a couple times with him still inside.

Keats finally crawled out feetfirst. "I'm coming, Henry!"

Dizzy, he staggered in the wrong direction, and then stumbled into Henry. His cousin was grinning at him. "You were really on a roll there, Keats," Henry said.

Something was bouncing around Henry's feet. It took a second for Keats to focus.

It was Mr. Cigam's toy dog!

"He survived the avalanche," Henry said. "He must have been following us."

The dog spun in small circles, yapping again and again.

Henry knelt down and held out his hand to the dog. "Hey, little guy, take it easy or you'll blow a fuse," he said. "What should we call him, Keats?"

Keats shrugged. He started to answer Henry when the toy dog leapt in the air and nipped at his fingers. Even with the little wrench still in its mouth, it hurt! So instead of "Fido," what came out of Keats's mouth was "Fi— Don't!"

Henry grinned. "Fidon't is a weird name, but I like it. What do you think, Fidon't?" The dog spun in more circles. "I wonder if he can do any other tricks."

"I don't know if spinning is really a trick," Keats said.

"This one might save us time." Henry waved his index finger at the dog. "Find a shortcut, Fidon't."

The toy dog wiggled like he was shaking off robot fleas. When Henry repeated "Find a shortcut," Fidon't scratched his tin ear with a hind leg.

"Too bad," Keats said. "Looks like we'll just stay on the—"

"Yap!" Fidon't interrupted. Then he took off, bouncing faster than ever on his spring legs.

The cousins watched him go for a second.

"Well, what are we waiting for?" Henry said. "Follow that toy!"

5

TUNNEL OF TROUBLE

HENRY AND KEATS chased after the dog as he bounded down the path.

Twice Fidon't wandered off into junk that had fallen from the walls. He chose the trickiest route through the heaps. The cousins had to pick their way behind him like mountain goats.

After a couple minutes of this, Keats started to doubt Fidon't.

"I think he's toying with us," Keats muttered as his sneaker got stuck between a concrete ramp and a canoe.

Up ahead, Fidon't did backflips like he thought this was hilarious. Then he spotted the ramp, too. His marble eyes squinted, and he growled.

Keats freed his shoe and followed the toy's eyes. The ramp led to an open garage door in the middle of the wall of junk. Tire tracks went up the ramp and stopped inside the doorway. The space was dark, but Keats could see another big door on the far end.

"It might be some kind of tunnel," Keats said.

Henry pumped his fist. "Yes! It's a shortcut!" he said. "We won't have to go all the way around the junkyard. We can cut through. Come on!"

Keats hesitated. "The Cigam sisters said to stay on the path," he reminded Henry.

"They also told us we'd be safe from the flying hog," Henry said.

"Good point," Keats said. He followed Henry into the tunnel.

But Fidon't didn't seem to like the idea. He crouched at the entrance and yapped louder than ever. The sound bounced off the metal walls. Keats winced, thinking about the hog.

"Fidon't!" he said. "Shhh!"

The dog spit the toy wrench out of his mouth. He leapt into the air and his teeth latched on to Keats's jacket.

"Hey!" Keats shouted. The dog tugged so hard that he tore a piece off Keats's sleeve. Fidon't ran to the middle of the path and shook the cloth in his mouth. His yapping was muffled but still loud.

Then Keats saw his fear coming true. A shadow streaked over the junk wall behind Fidon't.

"The junkyard hog is coming!" Henry said. "It must have heard the racket!"

"Watch out, Fidon't!" Keats said. The toy dog yapped one last time and ran off down the path. On the ground, the hog's shadow got larger.

Henry yanked Keats inside the tunnel. "Close the door!" he said. Henry jumped up to grab the lip of the garage door. He pulled, but it didn't budge.

Meanwhile, outside, the shadow was getting nearer.

Why is the hog still coming? Keats panicked. *We aren't using magic!*

He spotted the answer. The bag with the wand had opened slightly when Henry jumped

for the door. Keats reached over and zipped it up. Not soon enough.

"Yooodooohooo!" the hog yodeled from above. Keats knew what that meant. It was about to dive-bomb.

Keats pulled on the door, too. Groaning, the cousins put all their weight into it. The door slowly clattered down. It locked into place with a loud *kerklunk*.

Henry and Keats were now in the pitch dark.

Wham! The hog hit the outside of the door.

"Ahhh!" Keats yelled. The cousins stumbled back into the blackness of the tunnel. Keats pressed the button on the side of his watch, and its dim light came on.

In the glow, they saw the dull gleam of the metal walls. Henry walked slowly to the door.

"There isn't even a dent," Henry said. "It's made of really strong steel." He pressed his ear up against the door. "I don't hear anything."

"The hog must have gone after Fidon't," Keats said. "I hope the little guy is okay."

"I hope *we're* okay!" Henry said. He ran his hand along the door. "I don't see any handle. There's no way to open it!"

Keats blinked. Was he imagining it, or was the light from his watch starting to fade?

"Come on. Come on," Keats said, tapping the face of the watch. Soon it flickered like a sick firefly.

"Maybe the batteries just need some more power," Henry said. "We can use that wand-less spell."

Keats didn't like messing around with magic. But who wanted to be stuck in a dark room?

"Okay," he said. He held his watch near his face. *"Better bet this battered battery will be better yet."*

A sizzling sound and—

Fzzzt!

Light shot from his watch! The beam cut through the darkness. It made Keats feel like he had a lighthouse on his wrist.

"See?" Henry said. "Using magic is a good thing!"

Wazunk! The metal floor under their feet shuddered.

"What is that? An earthquake?" Keats asked. A whirring sound came from the walls, like a motor had just started.

Henry gave Keats a funny look. "Hey, are you getting bigger?"

Keats flashed the light around to each of the four walls. They were moving. "No," he said. "The room is getting smaller!"

When they'd first entered the room, it had been as long as a bus. Not anymore. Now Keats understood why the car tracks stopped in the middle of the space. Cars drove in. But they didn't drive out.

"This isn't a tunnel!" Keats said. "It's a car crusher! It smashes cars into little cubes!"

Henry's eyes widened as he got it. "And we just turned it on with that spell," he said. "We have to get out of here!"

"Try the other door!" Keats said. They dashed to the far end. The handle on that door was missing, too. A bolt stuck out instead. It was like a window crank without the handle.

Keats tried to turn it. No luck.

"We need the wrench from Fidon't," Henry said, looking around the room.

Keats pointed his watch around the space. Finally he spotted the wrench. "There!" One of the side walls was just sliding over it.

Henry dove and snatched up the wrench before it vanished under the moving wall. He put the wrench around the bolt and turned it once. The door rose half an inch.

"Hurry!" Keats said. A side wall pushed into his shoe.

"I'm trying!" Henry said. The door crept up another inch, and then another. Light and fresh air flowed into the space. Keats could see a ramp on the other side.

Henry turned the wrench two more times. The door had lifted about a foot off the ground. That would have to be enough. The room was the size of a shower stall and still shrinking.

"Quick!" Keats yelled.

He squeezed through the gap. Henry followed, but halfway through, he shouted, "I'm stuck!"

The backpack was jammed inside the door. Henry slid his arms out of the straps. He squirmed under the door until he was next to Keats on the ramp.

Henry reached back into the shrinking space.

"No, Henry!" Keats yelled.

"The wand is in there!" Henry said. He plucked the backpack free just as the walls slammed together with a *bang!* The crusher's machinery wound down and stopped.

The cousins lay on the ramp, sucking in air.

"Whoa," Henry gasped.

"That was way too close," Keats said. He sat up, his heart still pounding. Where were they now? Were they by the exit?

Rusted metal cubes sat in the dirt at the bottom of the ramp. It looked like the crusher had taken them to a large circle made by a wall of junk.

"Uh-oh," Keats said.

"What is this place?" Henry said.

Keats shook his head. "We're in the one spot the sisters told us not to go," he said. "We're in the center of the junkyard."

6

CAR GRAVEYARD

THE COUSINS CLIMBED to their feet. Henry slipped on the backpack.

"It looks like a stadium," Henry said as he stared out at the circle. "Or a place where gladiators fought."

Keats's eyes ran along the solid wall of junk. He was searching for a gap or a door. In the center of the circle, a crane sat on a platform by bins of parts.

"The crusher is the only way in and out of here," Keats said. Panic made his heart race. "And now that way is shut. We're trapped! We'll be easy pickings for the junkyard hog!"

"Easy, cuz," Henry said. He stared at the cubes lined up in rows between them and the crane. "Those are cars, right?"

"I guess," Keats said. "Or they were before the crusher squashed them."

"Yes!" Henry said, pumping his fist in the air.

Keats groaned. "You're excited about being trapped in a car graveyard?"

"You got it!" Henry cheered. "You told the sisters yourself. Your dad uses a compass in his . . ."

"In his car?" Keats said. He still wasn't sure where this was going.

Henry nodded. "Think about it. In every

section of the junkyard, the extra parts have been taken off and thrown into bins." He pointed to the bins in the center of the circle. "Those are the parts from the cars. If your dad has a compass in his car, maybe other people did, too!"

Now Keats was excited. "I didn't think of that!"

Henry laughed. "You're not the only genius on the team."

"All we have to do is get the compass. We stop the needle and *blammo!* The sisters will come and get us!" Keats said.

The cousins dashed to the bins, past the cubes of crushed cars. Keats shivered. He knew the cubes were just hunks of metal. But there was something creepy about them.

When they made it to the crane, Henry pulled himself up over the edge of the platform. He reached back down to help Keats. The bins on the platform were taller than any others they'd seen in the junkyard. Keats tried peeking inside one, but it was too full of parts for him to see everything.

"Hmmm," Keats said. "There's a door on the side of each bin. . . . What if . . . ?"

"Great idea!" Henry was already moving. He lifted the latch on a door of one bin and swung it open. Hubcaps poured onto the platform.

"No compasses here," Henry said. "Let's try another one."

The next bin was filled with headlights. The one after that held steering wheels. Finally there was only one bin left.

Keats crossed his fingers. If they didn't find the compass, they'd be trapped here.

Henry pulled the last door open and

everything inside tumbled out. Rearview mirrors. Sun visors. Door locks. Handles. And—

"Compasses!" Henry and Keats shouted at the same time.

All sorts of compasses clattered onto the platform and spilled over the side. Several had cracked glass domes. A few had black square cases. One was gold.

This last one caught Keats's eye. It tumbled off the edge of the platform and landed on one of the car cubes below.

Keats leaned over the side of the platform for a better look. This compass was shaped like a pineapple. It had a long chain and a shark carved on its lid. "That must be it!" he yelled.

Henry gave Keats a high five. "It's definitely weird enough to belong to the Cigams."

Keats and Henry jumped down from the platform onto the car cube. The compass

shook as they landed. Its lid popped open and a puff of air blew at them.

"Phew!" Henry held his nose. "Oh man, that's foul."

"Is that mothballs?" Keats said, wrinkling his nose. "Oh no." His stomach flip-flopped. "It smells just like the mixed-up magic from Mr. Cigam's house."

"You're right!" Henry said. "Maybe air from Hallway House was trapped inside the compass!"

Keats knew how fast mixed-up magic could spread. That meant . . .

"Everything is about to get nutty," Henry finished his thought for him.

As if it heard him, the cube under the compass jerked forward a few feet. Then, with a rattling noise, it started sliding across the dirt.

"Grab the compass!" Henry shouted.

He and Keats jumped down, and they chased after the cube. They were getting closer when—

"Yooodooohooo!" A yodel cut through the air.

Before they knew what was happening, a blur of movement crossed their vision.

Whoomp! The hog crash-landed next to the cube twenty feet from the cousins. The hog snorted and sniffed. With a happy squeal, it lowered its head and speared the chain of the compass around one tusk.

"No!" Keats shouted.

Without even glancing at Henry and Keats, the hog beat its wings and took off. In a second, it was airborne and heading out of the junkyard.

7

CATCH THAT HOG

FOR A MOMENT, Keats was too stunned to speak. The junkyard hog had the compass!

Meanwhile, as the air from Mr. Cigam's house spread, more car cubes were waking up. They made weird revving noises like they were about to race. One slid through the dirt and banged into Henry's leg.

"Ow!" Henry yelped. "Retreat! Back to the platform—now!"

Dodging the cubes, the cousins raced to the crane platform and pulled themselves up.

"If the hog leaves with the compass, the sisters will be dizzy forever," Keats said. "And we'll never get out of here!"

A ladder welded to the side of the crane caught Keats's eye. He climbed a few rungs up and called, "Sooooieeee!"

The hog got smaller and smaller as it flew farther away. It didn't even slow down.

"Hog calling was worth a try," Henry said. "But I've got another idea." He unzipped the backpack. "The wand! If I wave it, the hog might come back. You can grab the compass off his tusk, and we'll be set."

"*What?*" Keats couldn't believe his ears. "That's your World's Greatest Plan?"

"No." Henry shrugged. "I never said it was *great*." He wasn't scratching his chin. He was telling Keats the truth. "It's just a plan."

"I've got a bad feeling about this," Keats moaned.

Henry started waving the wand.

Keats squinted to track the hog. "It's not stopping!" he said.

"Go higher," Henry said. Keats pushed aside the crane's chain and climbed three more rungs. Henry stepped up behind him on the ladder.

"How about now?" Henry asked.

"Still no . . . ," Keats said. "Wait a second!" The flying hog had slowed down. Then it wheeled around.

"Here it comes!" Keats said.

"I knew it couldn't resist the smell of magic," Henry said. "It'd be like you saying no to a book!"

The hog crossed the space back to the

platform in seconds. It swept in low, sniffing the air. Henry moved the wand more slowly. "Wow," he said. "This is a stunner of a bad idea."

Keats couldn't have said it better himself. He almost hoped the junkyard hog wouldn't take the bait.

On the next pass, the hog dove lower. It opened its mouth and chomped down on the wand!

"Ah!" Henry's arm jerked up with the wand. "Now, Keats!" he shouted.

Keats grabbed for the compass. But the hog's wings flapped in his face. Its hooves knocked into his hand. And the super swine stench made him gag. Plus, the crane's chain swung back and forth between him and the hog.

"I can't get it!" Keats shouted.

Henry groaned as the hog pulled harder. He had one hand on the ladder and the other on the wand. Keats could see him straining to keep his grip.

"Let it go!" Keats said. "Or you'll fall!"

"No!" Henry said. "I won't let the hog have the wand *and* the compass!"

Keats reached out again, but the chain was still in the way. Wait! Maybe the chain wasn't *in* the way. Maybe it was *the* way. He looped an arm around a ladder rung and wrapped the chain around the hog's leg.

"Henry!" Keats shouted. "Let it have the wand!"

"You sure?" Henry said.

Keats nodded. "Trust me!"

Henry let go and grabbed the ladder with both hands.

With the wand in its mouth, the hog flew

higher into the air. But it didn't get far. The chain around its leg pulled tight. Like a fish on the line, the hog was jerked back down.

Flapping its wings furiously, the hog struggled to get free. The crane rocked as it pulled even harder.

Twenty-five feet above the cousins, the hog flew in circles. Its small red eyes burned as it followed the chain down to the cousins. Keats could almost read its thoughts: "Oh! *You* did this to me!"

For the first time, the hog seemed to really notice them.

And it was angry.

With its teeth still clamped down on the wand, the hog made a squealing sound—

ZAP!

A lightning bolt shot out of the end of the wand.

"Watch out!" Henry shouted.

The bolt hit one of the car cubes next to the platform. Sparks flew and the cube flipped over.

Before Henry and Keats could move, there was another squeal and another *ZAP!* That bolt just barely missed them. The junkyard hog seemed to be getting more and more furious.

"We have to hide!" Keats shouted. He and Henry scrambled down the ladder.

Instead of running away, though, Henry pulled Keats to an open part of the platform.

"What are you doing?" Keats cried.

"We need the hog to give up the wand," he said. "And there's only one way to do it. We have to be the bait!"

Before Keats could stop him, Henry waved his arms. "Here we are!" he yelled.

Hovering overhead, the hog glared down at them. It seemed to be taking aim.

"It's going to zap us, Henry!" Keats cried.

"Or dive-bomb!" Henry said with a wink.

A-ha! Now Keats could guess what Henry had planned. He waved his arms, too.

The hog's lips curled into a sneer. Then it opened its mouth to give a warning yodel—

"Yooodooohooo!"

—and the magic wand fell out.

"Yes!" Henry pumped his fist. The wand tumbled end over end. Keats snatched it from midair. The cousins had the wand!

The junkyard hog rocketed toward them.

"Duck!" Henry yanked Keats to the side. *Ker-klang!* The hog slammed into the platform where Keats had been standing.

With a snort, the hog sprang onto its hooves. It tried to nudge the chain off its leg using its snout. But the chain held fast. Giving up, the hog climbed back into the air for another pass. Keats had the feeling it wouldn't miss again.

"Make up a spell, Keats!" Henry urged. "We have about a second before we end up as hog pancakes."

Keats held out the wand. Panic filled his head. Finally he said, "Halt . . . that thing."

Nothing. No reaction from the wand.

"Say something that rhymes!" Henry said. He grabbed the wand from Keats.

"I'm not sure I can." Keats groaned. He couldn't stop watching the hog. "It's too hard to think right now!"

Henry flicked his shoulder. "You're the king of words, Keats," he said. "If a yodeling pig with wings can work the wand, I bet you can, too!"

Keats had to laugh. He felt his brain unfreeze.

"Yooodooohooo!" the hog yodeled again. It was ready to dive-bomb. But Keats didn't freak out. The words clicked into place.

As Henry waved the wand, Keats said, "Make this hog more safe for us. I really hate pickled asparagus!"

It was a goofy rhyme. Even Henry seemed

shocked. "That's it?" he said. "Did you say *aspara*—?"

BLA-BLIP!

A bright lightning bolt shot out of the wand. And the cousins were knocked off their feet.

8

ALL THE WAY HOME

KEATS SAT UP as the bolt crackled through the air. It split into two beams and blasted into the hog.

Zap! Zap!

The hog stopped in midair. Its white tusks turned dark green. And then, like two leaky balloons at a birthday party, they started to droop.

"The tusks are—" Keats couldn't believe it.

"They're pickled asparagus!" Henry said.

As the tusks shrank, the magical items slid off. The flying charm came loose first. It fell fifteen feet and shattered on the platform next to a pile of rusty tools. A jeweled bracelet, a diamond necklace, and a silver hoop earring also tumbled to the ground.

Then the compass slid off.

"Don't let it break!" Keats yelled.

Henry cupped his hands and easily caught the compass.

The hog's entire body seemed to deflate. As its body got smaller, the chain slipped off its leg.

Its wings were shrinking, too. The hog's red eyes went wide as it dropped lower and lower.

Then *flink! flink!* The wings disappeared completely. The hog bounced onto the platform next to the cousins.

It opened its snout to yodel.

". . . yoodoo," it squeaked.

The hog looked confused.

"Not so tough now, are you?" Henry asked.

The junkyard hog squeaked one last time. Then it leapt off the platform and ran away, darting between the cubes of cars.

"Where's it going?" Keats wondered.

"That little piggy?" Henry said with a grin. "Probably all the way home."

"It might be able to squeeze through the junk to get out," Keats said. "But we're still trapped."

They looked at the compass in Henry's hand. The needle was spinning around and around.

Keats felt woozy just watching it. "What should we do?" he asked.

"The sisters said to stop the needle from spinning," Henry said.

Keats tried to put his index finger on the needle. But he completely missed.

"Um," Henry said. "Keats, that's my wrist."

"Sorry," Keats said. The twirling compass was making him loopy. He aimed his finger again and got Henry's ear. On the third try, Keats finally jabbed the needle. It wiggled under his touch.

The needle slowed down. But now the compass case started to turn.

"Whoa," Keats said. He felt even more wobbly as the case picked up speed.

"It's squirmy, but I think I've got it," Henry said. He grabbed the case tighter. "Press harder, Keats!"

With a grunt, Keats did, and . . .

The needle stopped.

Pffft! A billowing purple cloud exploded on the platform. Then Beatrice and Lillian stood in front of them. Their hair and clothes were as wild as ever, but they were smiling.

"Hello!" Lillian cried.

"My sister means *Olleh*," Beatrice said, and then laughed. "Wait! Never mind! She can talk forward again. Thanks to you gentlemen!"

Beatrice took the compass from Henry while Lillian blew the cousins kisses. Henry pretended to duck, chuckling. "You're not dizzy anymore?" he asked.

"Some people will always call us dizzy,"

Lillian said. "But yes, we have our sense of direction back."

Keats and Henry high-fived. "Another satisfied customer, cuz!" Henry said.

"How did you know where to find us?" Keats asked the sisters.

Beatrice grinned. "Why, your friend let us know, of course."

"Friend?" Henry said.

Beatrice and Lillian stepped apart, and the cousins looked down. On the ground between the women's feet was a bouncing toy dog.

"Fidon't!" Henry shouted.

The dog's spring tail waved back and forth. And he did two high backflips. Keats crouched to pat his head. Fidon't spit out the piece of Keats's jacket like a present.

"Don't worry, he'll have a good home with us," Lillian said. "And now we can zap us all out of here."

"*Zap* us out of here?" Henry repeated, startled.

"Or we can give the compass a spin and see where it takes us!" Beatrice said.

Keats didn't like the sound of that, either. "If it's okay," he said, "we'd rather not travel by magical cloud or pineapple compass."

"Very well," Lillian said, and waved her hand. The cube cars around them went still. Beatrice waved a hand, too, and the doors to the crusher rose. The cousins could leave the junkyard now.

"Ah, that felt good," Lillian said, giggling. "We have some of our magic back, my dear Beatrice!"

Keats nodded at Henry. The sisters were going to be fine. "Thanks for the job," Henry said as they started off.

"Gentlemen, wait!" Beatrice called. "We can't give you money. We used all of our funds to buy this junkyard."

"That's okay, really!" Keats said.

"But as payment for a job well done," Lillian said, "please take one of the magical objects the hog left."

The cousins looked at the small heap of

charms and jewels that had fallen off the hog's tusks. They glittered next to the old tools.

"Holy moly." Keats whistled. "Which should we pick?"

"I've got it!" Henry answered. "We'll let luck decide." He covered his eyes with one hand. With the other hand, he plucked something out of the pile.

Keats couldn't wait to see what it was. Would it be something to help with their next magical job?

Henry turned and held out his hand. It was a rusty wrench.

Keats laughed. Henry groaned. And Fidon't started yapping with joy.

"Your friend is saying, *Excellent choice*," Beatrice told them.

Fidon't kept barking. Finally Keats gave Henry a nudge.

"Okay, okay." Henry chuckled. "It's all yours, Fidon't!"

He tossed the wrench. It spun through the air across the junkyard. Fidon't chased after it, bouncing happily all the way.

LOOKING FOR MORE MONSTER-FILLED FUN?
BE SURE TO READ

ATTACK
OF THE
SHARK-HEADED
ZOMBIE

ABOUT THE AUTHOR

BILL DOYLE grew up in Michigan and wrote his first story—a funny whodunit—when he was eight. Since then, he's written other action-packed books for kids, like *Attack of the Shark-Headed Zombie, Stampede of the Supermarket Slugs,* the Scream Team series, the Crime Through Time series, and the Behind Enemy Lines series. He lives in New York City with two treat-hogging dachshunds.

You can visit him online at billdoyle.net.

MORE MAGIC AND MAYHEM!

Find your next chapter book adventure at SteppingStonesBooks.com!

RHCB

STEPPING STONES